Ju
F
Si 6   Singer, Isaac Bashevis.
          Alone in the wild
       forest.

Ju
F
Si 6   Singer, Isaac Bashevis.
          Alone in the wild
       forest.

ALONE
IN THE WILD
FOREST

Isaac Bashevis Singer

PICTURES BY

Margot Zemach

TRANSLATED FROM THE YIDDISH

BY THE AUTHOR AND ELIZABETH SHUB

AN ARIEL BOOK

Farrar, Straus & Giroux

NEW YORK

Text © 1971 by Isaac Bashevis Singer

Pictures © 1971 by Farrar, Straus & Giroux, Inc.

All rights reserved

Library of Congress catalog card number: 78–161372

ISBN 0-374-30238-3

Published simultaneously in Canada by Doubleday Canada Ltd., Toronto

Printed in the United States of America

First printing, 1971

Designed by Cynthia Krupat

ALONE
IN THE WILD
FOREST

LONG AGO, in the days of the saintly Bal Shem, there lived a childless couple. Husband and wife consulted many rabbis and miracle workers, but no one could help them. The husband was no longer young, and more than anything else he wanted a son to recite the Kaddish prayer after his death.

He had heard that Bal Shem could do what others could not and went to seek his advice. When at last he entered the holy man's chambers, Bal

Shem looked at his petitioner with sadness and said: "Are you prepared to forfeit years of your life in return for a son?"

"I am prepared to die at once for a son," the man replied.

"But why? Without a father, your son will have a difficult life, especially while he is growing up."

"I am ready, nevertheless."

"Return home," Bal Shem said. "In time, your wife will bear you a son. Name him Joseph, because his trials and temptations will be as great as those of Joseph, the son of the patriarch Jacob."

Everything happened as Bal Shem had predicted. The man's wife bore him a son and he was named Joseph. When the boy was old enough, he was sent to cheder. But, from the beginning, the other children teased him and made sport of him. Joseph had no friends and seldom played with his

schoolmates. He seemed always to be brooding about something, and the boys would ask: "What are you worrying about? Are you afraid the sky will collapse and the moon will fall into the river?"

"He's dreaming awake," the teacher would remark.

"Let's not disturb him," the children would whisper, and titter among themselves. Or some boy would say in a taunting tone: "What's he dreaming of? A princess with golden hair?"

The Joseph of old, the Bible tells us, loved to relate his dreams, but our Joseph would not reveal his. He was afraid that his schoolmates would make fun of him. He often had strange experiences. Sometimes he heard people speak and it seemed to him that he had heard their words before. Once he visited a distant village with his father, and it was as familiar to Joseph as his own. He recognized each house, each alley. When they reached the marketplace, Joseph said: "Why have they removed the horse trough?" His father looked at him in astonishment. There had been a horse trough in the marketplace but it had been removed before Joseph was born. "How do you know that there was a trough here?" his father asked. Joseph could not reply.

In Joseph's village, there was an old man who spent his days studying the mysteries of the cabala, the ancient books that teach the secrets of creation. The boy and the old man became friends. The old man told Joseph that the souls of dead men are reborn to make amends for sins and injustices committed during their previous lifetimes. As a rule, these reborn souls have no memory of previous lives. But it happened that an exceptional soul could recollect events that had occurred in a former existence.

Alone in the Wild Forest

When Joseph reached fifteen, his father suddenly became ill and died, and soon afterward so did his mother. His parents left him no inheritance and Joseph was forced to look for work. He heard that a boy was needed at an inn on the outskirts of the village. Joseph went to the inn and applied for the post. The innkeeper, who was well known for his greed and dishonesty, hired the boy at a salary of two gulden a week. For this pittance, Joseph chopped wood, carried water, and served the guests. The innkeeper often scolded him and even beat him. Although Joseph was to be paid each quarter, almost two years passed and the innkeeper had still paid him only a few gulden.

One afternoon when the innkeeper was away, Joseph rested for a bit in the yard. Two horses grazed nearby. Joseph heard one horse say to the other, "How much longer are you going to be a slave here?"

"Until I have paid off my debt," the other replied.

"Our boss," the first horse remarked, "owes money to so many people that he'll have to be a horse in more than one life. As a matter of fact," the horse continued, "he already owes this orphan here over two years' wages, and he will never pay him a penny."

At that moment, to his delight, Joseph realized that he was understanding the language of the animals. On the other hand, the fact that he would get nothing for all his years of toil made him despair, and he decided to run away. The inn was located on the outskirts of a thick and endless forest. It was through this forest that Joseph decided to make his way. He walked by day, and at night he would search out a hollow in an old tree and lie down to sleep. He ate berries, mushrooms, and whatever herbs he could find. On the fourth day he arrived at a clearing, in the middle of which was an open hearth. A man stood by the fire tending a kettle whose contents resembled boiling pitch.

When he saw Joseph, he said: "Go and gather some wood for the fire."

For a week Joseph remained with the stranger, who addressed him only to give him orders. Although he fed Joseph bread and water, Joseph never saw him eat anything. The black mass cooked and seethed day and night. Only when the Sabbath came did the man put the fire out. Joseph soon realized that his master must be a creature of another world and that he was his prisoner.

One night, as Joseph lay sleeping, an angel appeared to him and said: "Joseph, my son, ask no questions, but do as I bid you. There is a thin branch lying near you. Dip it into the kettle. When it is well coated, take it with you and leave at once. The cook is sleeping soundly and will not hear you. If you are in need, call me and I will come to your aid.'' Then the angel disappeared.

Joseph did as the angel bade him. He dipped the branch in the black mass and with it disappeared into the dark forest. He heard the growling of beasts and the screeching of birds of prey. At first the branch he carried felt light against his shoulder. But the farther he went, the heavier it became. Soon he could barely carry it. After a while he became so tired he could not take another step. He remembered the angel's words to call him if he needed help, and he did so.

"Holy angel, I can no longer carry this weight. What am I to do?"

No sooner had he spoken these words than the angel appeared before him.

Alone in the Wild Forest

"My son, your employer was a devil," the angel said. "He was boiling captive souls in his kettle, and when you dipped your branch into it, many souls managed to cling to it. As you went along, the souls of their dead relatives came to greet them and they caught hold as well. That is why the branch became so heavy. Now give it to me and I will carry these souls to Paradise. And because you have helped me save them, I will give you this small bag made of parchment, containing an incantation written by Ezra the Scribe. It will bring you whatever you desire, but you must show it to no one and never reveal that you have it."

With these words, the angel took the branch from Joseph and flew away.

By daybreak Joseph reached a brook. He washed his hands, took the bag of parchment from his pocket, and said: "Little amulet, give me a prayer book." And at once Joseph held a prayer book in his hands.

When he had finished praying, Joseph said: "Please give me something to eat." A tray immediately appeared bearing fresh rolls, butter, cheese, an omelet, and a large bowl of milk. Joseph made the benediction, ate, and thanked God. Then he lay down on the grass and fell asleep.

At noon he awoke rested and said: "Little amulet, please give me my midday meal." And, as before, a tray appeared, this time laden with freshly baked bread, a plate of chicken broth with noodles, meat, stewed prunes, cookies made of egg dough, and tea. After praising the Lord for his bounty, Joseph said: "Little amulet, I'm lonesome; give me someone to talk to." This time a voice replied: "That, Joseph, is something you must seek and find for yourself."

Alone in the Wild Forest

Having rested and eaten, Joseph continued on his way. He met wild animals but they did not harm him. After walking a considerable distance, he stopped, took out his amulet, and said: "Please, give me an eagle to carry me wherever I am destined to go." He had no sooner finished speaking than a huge eagle alighted near him. On the eagle's back was a saddle from which hung silver stirrups. Joseph mounted the eagle and they flew without stopping for three days and three nights. The amulet supplied him with food and drink. At night Joseph slept but the eagle continued flying over mountains, valleys, seas, and rivers.

On the fourth day the eagle landed on the outskirts of a large city. As soon as Joseph dismounted, the eagle vanished, and Joseph went into the city. He found himself in the midst of lively streets lined with large buildings, palaces, and parks. The passers-by were richly dressed and spoke gaily in a language Joseph did not understand. He put his hand on the amulet and said: "Let me understand this strange tongue."

His wish was immediately granted. He saw a group of young men talking and laughing merrily. He walked over to them and asked: "What city is this? And why is everybody so happy?"

One of the young men replied: "This is the capital of Good King Maltuch's land. Our king had a huge treasure, which he spent to improve the country and make his people happy. He has an only daughter, the Princess Chassidah, the most beautiful girl in the world. Yesterday he let it be known that he would give her in marriage to the man who could refill his treasury with gold. This is good, for two reasons: first, Chassidah is heiress to the throne, and marriage will provide her with a consort to

help her rule when she is queen; second, when the king's treasury is replenished, he will have money to spend on even greater benefits for his subjects."

"What does Chassidah look like?" Joseph asked.

"Her skin is as silk, her eyes are blue as the sky, and her hair is golden," replied one of the group.

The king's palace was pointed out to Joseph and he went there. He told the guards that he had come as a suitor for the hand of Princess Chassidah. Although the guards had their doubts, they had orders to bring every suitor into the presence of the king, and so Joseph was escorted to him.

The king questioned Joseph: "Where is your gold? On a ship? In a caravan?"

"I have it here with me," Joseph replied.

"Enough gold to fill my treasury!" the king said in amazement. "As far as I can see, your pockets look empty."

"Your majesty, leave me alone in any chamber of your palace and I will fill it with gold."

The king did not believe Joseph. But he said good-naturedly: "Go into the next room, and let us see what you can do."

Joseph did as he was told and closed the door behind him. He took out his amulet and said: "Please, little amulet, fill this room with gold."

In one instant the room was filled with gold. It happened so quickly that Joseph was hardly able to get back through the door in time.

When the king and his courtiers saw what had happened, they were speechless. This young man was nothing less than a worker of miracles.

"I will keep my word," the king announced, "and give you my daughter in marriage." The king sent for Chassidah and she looked exactly as the young man in the street had described her. Her skin was as alabaster; her eyes were as blue as the sky; and her hair, which reached below her waist, was the color of spun gold. Her face had an expression of modesty and gentleness. When her father asked if she was willing to marry Joseph, she replied: "Yes, Father. It seems to me as if I have always known him."

Chassidah did not know that what she said was the truth. She had loved Joseph in a former life and through no fault of her own had been prevented from marrying him.

That night, with the help of his amulet, Joseph filled the king's treasury with gold. The date was set for the wedding, and the royal seamstresses began to work on the bride's trousseau. The royal builders started the construction of a new palace, where the young couple were to live.

However, the king's first minister, Bal Makane,

wanted to be the queen's consort after King Maltuch's death and for some time had been plotting to win Chassidah's hand.

Bal Makane sought her out and said: "When a man truly loves a woman, he has no secrets from her. Joseph used mysterious powers to fill the treasury with gold. You must test his love by asking him for his secret. If he does not divulge it, you will know that he is marrying you only because you are heir to the throne."

Chassidah did not realize that Bal Makane was trying to trick her. She sent for Joseph and said: "Tell me how you filled my father's treasury with gold. If you do not tell me, I will know that you do not love me."

In vain, Joseph insisted that he was forbidden to reveal his secret. Chassidah, sure that Joseph did not love her, began to weep. "Very well," Joseph

said, unable to bear her tears. "I will tell you everything, no matter what my punishment is." He
showed her the amulet and explained its powers.
The very same day Chassidah, to prove Joseph's
love, went to Bal Makane and told him about the
amulet.

⁓⁓⁓⁓

Bal Makane's famous palace was built on pillars
and extended out over the ocean. It had a secret
room with a trap floor that could be opened into the
sea. Bal Makane used this room to destroy his ene-
mies.

He invited Joseph and Chassidah to visit him.
After they had banqueted, he offered to show Joseph the palace while Chassidah rested in the gar-

den with her ladies. He took him to the secret room and, since the day was warm, suggested that Joseph remove his coat, which he handed to a footman. Bal Makane knew from Chassidah that Joseph carried his amulet in his coat pocket. As Joseph went from window to window admiring the view, Bal Makane left the room and ordered the trap floor to be opened. Within a second, Joseph had fallen into the sea. He tried to get back to shore, but the current was strong and pulled him farther and farther out. Joseph soon realized that the only way he could save himself from drowning was to let himself drift with the tide, and thus he managed to stay afloat until daybreak.

Bal Makane immediately sent word to the king that Joseph had disappeared before his very eyes. He pointed out that those who harness evil powers often fall victim to their own witchcraft. Bal Makane tried to make use of Joseph's amulet to acquire greater riches and more power, but it did not work for him and in anger he threw it into the furnace.

The current had carried Joseph to an island in the middle of the sea. When he finally reached the shore, he was exhausted and hungry. But the sun soon warmed and dried him. He found pineapples, pomegranates, and fruits he had never seen before, but no people. After eating his fill and drinking water from a stream, Joseph made his way into the interior of the island in search of its inhabitants. At last he came to a tower. It had a balcony on which stood a man in a dark cloak. His hair and beard were long and white. The sun was already setting and the moon and the first stars appeared in the sky. The old man studied the heavens through a spy glass. As Joseph approached, he motioned him to a door in the side of the tower. It opened onto a spiral staircase. The old man came to meet Joseph and led him to a circular room in which there were many old books, scrolls, and maps. He asked Joseph to be seated and brought him a cup filled with a strangely delicious drink. Night fell, but no oil lamp was lighted.

The old man said to Joseph: "My son, know that you are one of those souls that from the moment of birth have great forces striving for them and equally great forces working against them. The constellations show that fortune will soon be on your side. It has been revealed to me that you and Chassidah loved each other in another existence. You were led astray by a witch and deserted Chassidah, and she died of longing for you. You have both been returned to earth so that you, Joseph, could repay the debt of love due her. Rest overnight and in the morning I will tell you what to do."

Joseph slept, while the old soothsayer searched the heavens until dawn. When Joseph awoke, the sun had just risen. The old man took him out on the

balcony, talking for a long time and revealing to him many secrets. Then he pointed to a dense forest and said: "Make your way eastward through that forest until you reach the far shore of this island. When you arrive there, you will know what you are to do next." Joseph fell to his knees to thank the soothsayer, who bade him rise and embraced him in farewell.

After several hours of walking, Joseph reached a river. On its bank was a small rowboat tied to a species of tree he did not know. Joseph noticed that the boat had only one oar. The tree bore an odd fruit that resembled golden apples, and two of these apples were conversing. One of them said: "Whoever eats me will grow horns." The other replied: "Whoever eats me will lose those horns."

Joseph picked both apples and put them in his pocket. He untied the boat and got into it. He tried to use the oar as a paddle, but the boat began mov-

 33

ing of itself, and soon it had floated out into the open sea. This sea, however, was quite different from the one into which he had fallen from Bal Makane's palace. It was smooth and transparent. He could see into its depths, which abounded in strange plants and unusual fish. Its bed was covered with subterranean towns, castles, and parks. The fragrance of the air made Joseph think that the Garden of Eden must have smelled like this. He sailed by many islands, each one different from the others. On one island, all the inhabitants were occupied in prayer. All the people on another island were singing and dancing. A third island was inhabited only by children, all of whom seemed involved in some mysterious game. It was neither day nor night but a serene twilight. If only I could remain here forever, Joseph said to himself.

At that moment the scene changed and his boat

was sailing in a real ocean. There was a heavy wind blowing and the waves rose high. The little boat tossed and rocked and Joseph tried to steady it with his single oar. Joseph began to pray, "Merciful God, save me." Immediately the wind subsided. The boat arrived at a shore which was familiar to him. He had returned to the land where Chassidah's father ruled. The boat had come to rest near the palace of Bal Makane.

It was evening and the palace was brightly lit. There was a ball in progress. Joseph could hear music being played and in the gardens glimpsed men and women moving about in their festive clothes. A guard caught sight of Joseph's boat, came to the shore, and called: "Who are you? Where have you come from? How did you get here with only one oar?"

Instead of replying, Joseph asked: "What is happening at the palace?"

"My lord Bal Makane is giving a ball. Tonight the king is to announce the engagement of Crown Princess Chassidah and Bal Makane."

When Joseph heard these words, he was grief-stricken. He said to the guard: "Wasn't she betrothed to Joseph, the one who filled the king's treasury with gold?"

"He was a sorcerer, and the devil carried him away, no one knows where," said the guard. "But who are you? You cannot stay here unless you have an invitation to the ball."

"I'm a magician," Joseph replied. "Since there is a ball, I will perform my magic tricks and entertain the guests."

Alone in the Wild Forest

The guard sent word to Bal Makane that a magician had arrived in a one-oared boat and wished to entertain the guests.

Bal Makane was greatly astonished. The current around the palace was so strong that no rowboat could possibly have reached the shore. He decided that this magician must have unusual skill and ordered that he be permitted to enter the palace. As Joseph made his way through the palace gardens, he knew he must disguise himself, or Bal Makane would again try to kill him. He took the horn-growing apple from his pocket and bit into it. Two curved horns like those of a ram immediately sprouted from his forehead.

When Joseph appeared, there was great commotion. Some of the guests did not believe that his horns were real, and wanted to feel them. The king himself inspected them, and when he realized that they were not false, he asked Joseph to become his court fool. What could be more amusing than a fool with horns?

The ball grew noisier and gayer. The fiddlers played; the trumpeters blew; the flutists piped; and the drummers drummed. Bal Makane was delighted to be able to offer such unusual entertainment. Chassidah came over to the magician and drew him aside.

"Can't anything be done to rid you of those horns?" she said. "You would be so handsome without them. It's strange, but you resemble someone I love."

"Your highness," Joseph said, "if you love someone else, why are you marrying the First Minister?"

"My father insisted that I marry Bal Makane."

"Perhaps I can help you, Princess Chassidah."

"We can talk better," Chassidah said, "in the garden." As Joseph followed Chassidah out of the palace, he quickly took a bite of the other apple and in one second his horns disappeared. When Chassidah looked back, she cried out, "Joseph!"

"Yes," Joseph replied.

"But the horns . . ." Chassidah exclaimed in bewilderment.

Joseph told her everything that had happened. Chassidah burst into tears and said: "What am I to do now? I love only you."

"Chassidah, it is destined that you will be my wife," Joseph said. "And I know that tonight our fate is to be decided. Let us return to the ball."

Joseph took a bite from the first apple and the horns again appeared on his forehead. Together he and Chassidah went back into the palace. The horned magician had already been missed by the guests. Bal Makane had been looking for his betrothed. When he saw her with the magician, he could not curb his annoyance. "Why do you neglect our guests for that horned ox?" he said.

"Would your excellency still say that if, God forbid, you yourself grew horns?" Joseph asked.

"Why should I grow horns?" Bal Makane retorted. In a boasting tone, he continued, "I am First Minister, and I will soon be the king's son-in-law."

A servant came in carrying goblets of wine for the guests. Before Bal Makane could drink from his goblet, Joseph managed to slip a tiny piece of the horn-growing apple into it. Bal Makane had no sooner emptied his goblet than a pair of twisted horns appeared on his forehead. The ladies began to scream; the men gasped.

"What is this?" Bal Makane cried out in consternation, as he felt his forehead.

"Your excellency, we are now two of a kind,"

Joseph said. "Let us amuse the noble guests by having a bucking bout."

"He is a sorcerer, hang him!" Bal Makane screamed in rage. "He came here to turn us all into freaks. Guards! Soldiers!"

"I am not a sorcerer, but you, Bal Makane, are a murderer. It was you who had Joseph thrown into the sea. But he did not drown, for I am Joseph."

"You are Joseph! But Joseph had no horns," Bal Makane insisted.

"Neither do I," Joseph said and, taking the second apple from his pocket, he again bit into it. In an instant his horns had disappeared. Chassidah embraced Joseph, to the astonishment of all the guests.

"Bal Makane," the king said, "now that I know the truth, according to the law you should be hanged. But since we are gathered here today to celebrate an engagement—the engagement of Joseph and Chassidah—I do not wish to spoil the day with a hanging. I, therefore, exile you from this land. I order you to leave at once."

"Where can I go with a pair of horns on my head?" Bal Makane whimpered.

"That is no concern of mine," the king replied, turning away.

"Oh, I have earned my punishment," Bal Makane cried, appealing now to Joseph. "But you are a merciful man. Please free me of these terrible horns, and I promise to do only good from this day on."

"I would be glad to do so, if it depended on me," Joseph said. "But we die and are born again to correct our wrongdoing. At the last judgment all souls must be cleansed so that they may appear before God." Then he revealed what the soothsayer had told him. "In your former life, Bal Makane," said Joseph, "you were a brigand. You ambushed merchants in the forest, robbed and killed them. You were reborn to atone for your sins. Instead, you have sinned even more. This is what you must do. Seven days' travel from here, there is a forest in which lives a witch called Zlichah. You must go and find her. Take nothing more with you than will fit into a bundle that you can carry on your back. I can tell you no more, but the longer you delay, the worse your fate will be."

Bal Makane was desperate at having to give up Chassidah, his high office, his palace, wealth, and treasures to go in search of a witch. But when he saw that neither the king nor Joseph would change his mind, he packed some clothes and food in a bundle, covered his horns with a large hat, and set out.

That evening Joseph was betrothed to Chassidah for the second time. The wedding was postponed only long enough so that the most honored persons in the land could be invited. Word spread throughout the country that Joseph was a saintly man. The king immediately appointed him viceroy and entrusted him with all the secrets of the kingdom.

For three days Bal Makane walked in the direction of the forest, using only little-known paths, because he feared that someone might recognize him. After seven days of weary travel, he arrived at the foot of a steep mountain. It seemed to be one great rock. The sun was setting and the mountain reflected its scarlet light. A black cloud sat on the summit. Suddenly a stone door opened out of the mountainside, and there stood a being with the head of a pig, the body of an ape, and the feet of a giant frog. At the sight of this monster, Bal Makane was about to turn and flee. But before he could do so, it opened its snout and said: "Are you Bal Makane? I have been waiting for you. And why don't you remove your hat when a lady speaks to you? Weren't you taught any manners?"

In his fright, Bal Makane removed his hat. The monster clapped its paws together in delight, and said: "Well, well, my husband-to-be has horns."

"Are you Zlichah?" Bal Makane asked in consternation.

"Yes, I am Zlichah. This castle belongs to me, as do the hundreds of hobgoblins here who serve me. I have been waiting for you, my bridegroom, for many years. At last you have come, and you have such pretty horns. Don't be bashful. Come close to your Zlichah."

Instead of coming closer, Bal Makane began to back away, but Zlichah said: "Don't try to run away, my beloved. The road back is gone. Whoever comes here remains for good."

Bal Makane saw that he was trapped. The path along which he had come had truly disappeared. But he could not bring himself to come closer to Zlichah.

"What's the matter? Don't I please you?" Zlichah called in a shrill voice. "You and I are a perfect couple. We will have children that will combine our best qualities—meanness and cruelty. We will multiply like rabbits. Then we will make war on man and destroy him. The name of God will be forgotten. We will serve the King of all Kings, the Devil."

Although Bal Makane could not be called a good man, these words shocked him, and he replied: "I have come here to repent for my sins, not to commit new ones."

"Nonsense! The world belongs to the Devil and not to God."

Knowing that he must find any excuse for delaying this abominable marriage, Bal Makane said: "Zlichah, I will marry you, but not until a month from now. Since no human female ever loved me, I showered all my love upon a dog, who died just before I left. I must mourn her for at least thirty days. It will take me that long to recover from my loss."

When Zlichah heard these words, she howled with laughter. "Mourning a miserable dog," she roared. "I have all kinds of animals and often one of them dies or I kill one, but I couldn't care less. You may pick the best dog I have for yourself, or perhaps you'd prefer a wolf. I have a creature who was brought up by wolves but she resembles a human. Her name is Zeivah. If you like, I'll give her to you as a wedding present. Come, I will show her to you right now!"

Zlichah led the way into the mountain. Beyond the door was a huge courtyard. The mountain was hollow; up above, the sky could be seen. At one end of the yard was a kind of menagerie. Some of the animals were in cages; others were tied to posts. Some lay quietly, while others growled and howled. Suddenly Bal Makane caught sight of Zeivah. He saw at once that she was not an animal but a human girl, naked.

She had long hair and green eyes. Though she crawled on her hands and knees and bayed like a wolf, she was neither kept in a cage nor tied up.

"But she's human," Bal Makane cried out.

"A human brought up by wolves is no longer

human," Zlichah replied. "She eats raw meat and cannot speak. She is yours. Do with her as you wish. Now let us go and have something to eat."

Bal Makane was so hungry that he asked no questions but followed Zlichah. She led him into a cave which was filled with rabbits, calves, sheep, as well as pheasants and other birds, all black from roasting. Zlichah seated herself on a stool and motioned Bal Makane to join her. She tore a leg from a goose and handed it to him.

"Let's have some wine," Zlichah said. She clapped her paws and a weird creature appeared. It had the head, comb, and feet of a rooster but stood upright like a man. Two paws stuck out from among its feathers. It opened its beak and with a cawing voice asked: "What is my mistress's wish?"

"Tarnegol, this is my husband-to-be. Bring wine for both of us."

"At your service," Tarnegol crowed and went

off. Soon he returned, carrying two gourds filled with a dark liquid. Bal Makane accepted one of the gourds, but its smell was so pungent that he could not bring himself to drink of it.

"Your health, Bal Makane. Mazel tov. A year from today, we will drink to our newborn baby." Zlichah emptied the gourd in one gulp.

"Why aren't you drinking, Bal Makane?" Zlichah asked.

"Zlichah, my dear, I am not used to such strong wine."

"Just taste it, and I will finish the rest," she said, laughing.

Bal Makane brought the gourd to his mouth and pretended to take a sip. But the mere closeness of the liquid made his lips pucker.

He handed Zlichah the gourd and she gulped down its contents. Tarnegol looked on with disap-

proval. He blew himself up, his coxcomb turned dark red, and he crowed: "You've been drinking since morning, my mistress, and you know what the end will be." And he strutted out.

Zlichah ranted on. "I've been surrounded by demons, devils, goblins, hobgoblins, imps, and sprites, but what I've always longed for was a man. Now that I have you, we will bring forth a new race that will know the tricks of the devils and have the cunning of humans. We will rule the world."

Soon she began to clap her hands and call for Tarnegol and more wine. Tarnegol brought in another gourdful, but said: "Mistress, I warn you for the last time."

"You cursed rooster, don't tell me what to do," Zlichah screeched at him. She grabbed the gourd and gulped down the wine. She hiccuped, laughed, and fell face down on the ground. "Now you may be sure she'll sleep for days. Cock-a-doodle-do," Tarnegol crowed. He was about to leave, but Bal Makane motioned him to stay and whispered, "I want to talk to you. But not here. She may wake up."

"You can speak right here," Tarnegol replied. "After three gourdfuls of this wine, my mistress is dead to the world. This wine comes from Asmodeus's wine cellar. My mistress will sleep at least seven days and seven nights."

"What is this all about?" Bal Makane asked.

"All of us here were humans in a former life," Tarnegol explained. "Those of us who committed the greatest sins were sentenced to Zlichah's castle. In one of her lives, she caused the death of many people. I was once Meroduk X, the king of an island in the Indian Ocean. I had hundreds of wives, concubines, and slaves. I sacrificed many of my children to the idols we worshipped. As each of my wives reached her thirtieth birthday, I gave a banquet in her honor that lasted all night, and at dawn I had her beheaded.

"I expected to live a long life, but when I reached the age of forty, I became ill and no doctor could save me. After my death, the court built a pyramid in my honor. There I was placed in a golden coffin. Then they killed my wives, my concubines, and my slaves and buried them with me, believing that in this way they would insure for me the pleasures I had enjoyed during my lifetime.

"But the moment the pyramid was sealed, devils grabbed hold of me and carried me to that place in heaven where we are all judged. A giant scale stood there. On one side they placed my sins; and there were so many that the scale nearly toppled over. On the other side they set down my good works, which were few. And so I was sentenced to become the rooster Tarnegol, servant to Zlichah, the most vicious of witches."

When Bal Makane realized that he had won Tarnegol's confidence, he asked him about Zeivah. "I know very little about her," Tarnegol replied. "My mistress found her in the forest among wolves and brought her here. She speaks only the language of wolves, which I don't understand."

"I'd like to see her again," Bal Makane said. "Will you take me to her?"

"Since you are betrothed to my mistress, I must do as you ask," Tarnegol said.

"In that case, can you help me escape? I will take you with me, if you like."

Tarnegol uttered a sound which was a mixture of a laugh and a crow. "No one has ever escaped from my mistress," he replied. "But I can lead you to Zeivah since that was my mistress's will."

Alone in the Wild Forest

Before he followed Tarnegol to Zeivah, Bal Makane picked up a piece of meat to bring to her. Tarnegol left him almost immediately to join his wife, Tarnegoleth. Zeivah must have been starved, because she grabbed the meat and gobbled it up. Then she began to lick Bal Makane's hand.

During the seven days in which Zlichah slept, Bal Makane took her place as ruler of the castle. Tarnegol and Tarnegoleth and all the other devils were eager to serve him. But Bal Makane was no longer the power-greedy person he had once been. He became attached to Zeivah and hoped to be able to bring her back to human ways. On the seventh day, when Zlichah began to groan in her sleep and it looked as if she would soon awaken, Bal Makane packed a sack full of meat, called Zeivah, and made his way to the door through which Zlichah had brought him inside. The door was bolted on the inside and he opened it. He was out of the mountain and he had Zeivah for company. Although there was no path, he decided to make his way through the dense forest in a westerly direction.

Even though Bal Makane wasn't sure that what he had done was right, because he had been sent to Zlichah to expiate his sins, he decided he would rather perish than spend the rest of his life with that witch. He had been afraid that Zeivah would not follow him out of the castle, but she seemed quite willing to go with him, and he took this as a good omen.

They walked for many hours, and every step was made with difficulty. Bal Makane was constantly forced to push back branches and stumbled over roots and into mossy holes. Toward evening, he took some meat from his sack and fed Zeivah and himself.

When the sun had finally set and the crowns of

the trees turned purplish red, a deep sadness over-
came Bal Makane. Until that moment he had never
prayed to God; indeed, he had often blasphemed.
But for the first time in his life he had the desire to
pray.

He stopped and his words seemed to come of
themselves in a chant he had never heard before:
"Creator of heaven and earth, I have sinned heavily
against you, both in this life and in my former lives.
But my punishment is too heavy to bear. You gave
me the horns of an ox. I find myself alone in this
forest with a human daughter who is like a beast. I
am sorry for the sins I have committed and I pray
to you, Lord of the Universe, redeem me from my
suffering or let me die."

Bal Makane spoke these words with deep sin-
cerity, and strangely, Zeivah seemed to pray with
him, in her own way. Her mournful whimper ac-

companied his chanting. It seemed as if she too realized the misery of her existence and was imploring the Lord of the World to save her.

Zeivah had committed a terrible sin in her former life. She had promised her love to a poor young man but had married a rich man for his money. Her fiancé was so heartbroken that he left his village for the forest, where he was devoured by wolves. It was to atone for this sin that Zeivah had been reborn. At the age of three, she had been lost in a forest. A pack of wolves were about to tear her to pieces, but one of the wolverines prevented it and brought the baby up with her own whelps. That wolverine had been Zeivah's mother in a former life.

Bal Makane and Zeivah prayed together until the sky turned black and out of its blackness the stars appeared. Soon many other animals were chorusing Bal Makane's prayer. Wolves howled, bears growled, wild birds sang out mournfully. Bal Makane realized something that had never occurred to him before: all that exists prays. The entire earth, with all its rocks, plants, and creatures, prays to God. Prayer is the stuff that heaven and earth are made of.

When Bal Makane at last finished his supplications, he felt purified.

At that moment his forehead began to itch. He scratched himself and his right horn fell off. He rubbed his forehead again and lost his left horn. He prostrated himself on the ground and, crying with joy, thanked his Creator. Zeivah came to him and licked his forehead.

That night, as he had done on his way to Zlichah, he slept in the hollow of a tree. Zeivah made a bed for herself at the foot of the tree, ready to drive away anything that might attack her benefactor.

Bal Makane and Zeivah wandered through the

woods for many weeks, hoping to find the way back to the kingdom of Maltuch. The time was not wasted. Bal Makane began to teach Zeivah human language and how to walk upright. She learned quickly. Within two months she was behaving like a human. She became conscious of her nakedness, and Bal Makane made a dress for her out of leaves. Their meat supply was soon gone, and they nourished themselves with berries, mushrooms, and edible roots. As Zeivah changed, Bal Makane saw how beautiful she was, and he began to love her. And she loved him in return. Bal Makane decided that they would be married as soon as they reached a human community.

One day at dusk, when Bal Makane had already despaired of ever coming to the end of the forest, he saw towers and roofs in the distance. He recognized the city as the one in which he had lived and

where he had been the right hand of the king. From a long way off, he could hear the ringing of bells, the sound of trumpets, and the shouting of crowds. When Bal Makane and Zeivah reached the outskirts of the city, a man dressed in holiday clothes rushed by them. "What is happening?" Bal Makane asked.

The man looked with amazement at the half-naked pair and replied: "It is the wedding day of our beloved Joseph and the Crown Princess Chassidah. The honored guests have arrived from afar. The whole city is invited."

It was the custom in King Maltuch's country to give a beggars' feast on the day of a royal wedding.

There were no paupers in the kingdom, but some cripples, idlers, and poor travelers were gathered together and a banquet was prepared for them in the king's gardens. When the revelers saw the ragged and barefoot pair, they were overjoyed and led Bal Makane and Zeivah at once to the palace. They were seated at the table, which was laden with the most luxurious foods and rare wines.

At just about this time, Joseph and Chassidah stepped out from under the wedding canopy as man and wife. It was the custom for the royal couple to partake of their first meal at the banquet of the poor.

When the royal party arrived in the garden and saw Bal Makane and Zeivah, they were baffled. "Who are these wretched creatures?" the king called out. "Why were they not given some clothing?"

Bal Makane lowered his head and replied: "Your majesty, you do not recognize me. I am Bal Makane, and the girl beside me is called Zeivah. She is my bride-to-be. The Lord of the Universe, who is merciful even to sinners, has brought me home. Good luck to your majesties, to the royal couple, and to all the citizens of this happy country."

Everyone was so astounded that Bal Makane's words were met by a long silence.

King Maltuch was the first to speak. "Now I recognize you, Bal Makane. Since the Lord has helped you to return, welcome back. Your exile is at an end."

"Where have you been?" "How did you get back?" voices called.

"How did you manage to free yourself from Zlichah's clutches?" Joseph asked. And, without waiting for an answer, he added, "There can only have been one way: you have repented with all your heart. Only repentance could have saved you."

"Yes, my lord, I have repented with all my heart. I have seen both God's might and His mercy."

"Because you have truly repented," Joseph said, "your name must be changed. You will no longer be known as Bal Makane, the man of envy, but as Bal Tshuvah, the repentant one."

A few days later Bal Tshuvah and Zeivah were married. Joseph requested the king to permit the ceremony to take place in the royal gardens.

It was clear to everyone that the former Bal Makane was completely changed. There was an air of contentment about him, which only true love can create. Soon after, Joseph suggested to the king that Bal Tshuvah be appointed to a high office.

But Bal Tshuvah said: "Your majesty, I desire no office. What I would like is to tell our story

throughout the country, to show that no matter how deeply one falls into evil, the gates of repentance are always open."

"A man's will must be honored," Joseph said, quoting the Talmud.

Joseph and Chassidah lived happily, and when King Maltuch died after reaching a great age, Chassidah became queen and Joseph her consort and prime minister. The miraculous story of Bal Tshuvah and Zeivah spread throughout the land and was handed down through the generations. Those who met Zeivah could hardly believe that this lovely lady had once roamed the forest with a pack of wolves.

When the witch Zlichah awakened from her deep sleep and saw that her horned bridegroom had disappeared, she was so grieved that she started drinking again and continued until she died. The evil spirits escorted her soul to hell.

But even she will not remain there forever. All souls must be cleansed and at the End of Days appear before God, their Father. He has prepared for them a heavenly festival and the eternal joys of Paradise.